T0072309

THE BLACKER SIDE OF BUDDHISM

Harry J Blackwood

authorHOUSE®

AuthorHouse™ UK
1663 Liberty Drive
Bloomington, IN 47403 USA
www.authorhouse.co.uk
Phone: UK TFN: 0800 0148641 (Toll Free inside the UK)
        UK Local: (02) 0369 56322 (+44 20 3695 6322 from outside the UK)

Published by AuthorHouse   08/16/2023

ISBN: 979-8-8230-8429-1 (sc)
ISBN: 979-8-8230-8430-7 (e)

Introduction

Terry Johnson is a trouble shooter in the aviation industry working on business trips to the far east. Suddenly his driver said he had killed baby fetuses to make baby spirits go to work for him. 'We do it all the time said the driver.' 'How do you get a real baby?' Asked Terry. We pay a real women to get pregnant then after eight months have gone by, we make her have the baby. Then we put the baby on the roof in the sun and pray and chant over the baby for 40 days Then the baby spirit becomes ours, will work for us, and do anything we ask it to do. Even to harm someone. 'That's murder Sammy' (the drivers name). Terry Johnson was enticed into finding out more and went to Thailand to find out if he could stop it. But he would be placed in Danger by the Kuman Thong.

Chapter- One

Terry Johnson was a tall man of six feet four, good looking for his 65 years who worked out in the gym every day at dawn. with a long thin nose, a square jaw, plus dimples in his cheeks. He had a nice friendly smile. Terry was a successful businessman in the aviation industry selling Lear jets to corporations as well as rich Chinese individuals. He was on a month-long trip to the Lion City. After a long day at the office, he was now relaxing in the back seat of his air-conditioned chauffeur driven limo. Terry's trip only had six days to go, so he was looking forwards to going back to his home in Warwickshire England. He knew the driver of the limousine as Sammy who didn't have a lot going for him. He was a fat short man of only five foot tall. He was of Chinese origin and had slits for his black eyes, a flat nose, and thin lips. Terry would stop at a local bar for a few beers to unwind on his way back to the Hotel. Tonight, was one of those nights. After a few beers half-drunk he decided to leave the bar and head back to the hotel.

Later, on the way back to the Hotel Sammy the driver declared that he was a Buddhist and had been all his life. He spoke in broken English. Sir, are you interested in religion?' Terry wasn't interested in religious affairs and replied that no he wasn't into religion at all. Then the driver asked Terry if he was interested in ghosts at all? To which Terry replied, 'No I'm not interested in ghosts, and I don't believe in ghosts.'

Have you heard of the baby spirits?

'No, I haven't heard of the baby spirits what's that all about?'

'I've got five baby spirits working for me,' said the driver in a proud voice.

'What do you mean you've got five baby spirits working for you? asked Terry.

I'm saving my money up to buy a sixth baby spirit. The baby spirits do anything I want them to do for me sir.

'Like what?

'For one they make me prosperous.'

'For two they will protect me and attack my enemies if I want them to.'

Curious Terry asked the driver how he obtained these so-called baby spirits.

The driver looked at Terry in his rear-view mirror and spoke, 'well, for a start we must get a real baby to get its spirit.'

Yawning in boredom Terry said,

'How do you get a real baby Sammy.' Calling the driver by his first name.

The driver looked in the rearview mirror again and gave a cough then said, 'Well, first we must get a woman to get her pregnant. Then we wait until the woman is seven or eight months pregnant. Then we get the baby out of her. Terry interjected and said in an angry voice, 'You take the baby fetus from the woman at seven or eight months old. That's murder Sammy!'

'The woman is paid very well sir at the beginning of her getting pregnant.' Unperturbed, the black-eyed driver continued with his tale, 'then we put the baby in the hot sun to bake on the roof tops. Next, we pray and chant over the dead baby for forty days. Then we take that baby's spirit to work for us.'

Terry was angry with the driver and said again that what he was doing was an act of murder. The driver was unimpressed with his passenger's anger saying, sticking his chest out he said in a proud voice, 'You are a foreigner here! We Buddhists have been doing this ritual for years and years.'

Terry had one last question to ask the driver, 'So, you already have five baby spirits working for you. (that's five dead baby fetuses Terry thought) How many more do you want?'

'I want ten babies working for me in the future. I'm halfway there.'

That's five more murders, five more people's lives to be snuffed out like a candle. Where does this practice originate from Sammy?'

The driver turned his head towards Terry and said, 'In Bangkok, Thailand sir.'

Terry didn't sleep well that night thinking about the babies murdered by the driver and no doubt his friends too. He thought about reporting it to the city police. But what could they do? These women were paid cash for their babies in advance and doing this of their own volition. He was thinking how he could put a stop to this horrific practice, or at least raise some kind of public awareness about these atrocities. It originated in Bangkok Thailand, that much he knew. He wondered how he could stop this practice. Maybe he could go to

Thailand, talk to the right people at the top and those poor women at the bottom of the food chain, the ones who gave up their babies for what would amount to a few hundred pitiful dollars for a life. He decided to go to Thailand and find out more about this abominable practice. He wondered what his work would have to say about his upand-coming trip to Thailand although he had some time off owed to him, he didn't know how long it would take. He couldn't stand by and watch while hundreds of babies were being sacrificed. He knew he had to do something about it but what?

Chapter-Two

Buddhism is one of the most respected of religions in the world. It is also one of the world's largest religions and originated 2,500 years ago in India. Buddhists believe that the human life is one of suffering, meditation, spiritual physical labour, and good behavior are the ways to achieve enlightenment or nirvana.

Buddhism is a religion that is based on the teachings of Siddhartha Gautama. The main principals of this belief system are karma, rebirth, and impermanence. Buddhists believe that life is full of suffering, but that suffering can be overcome by attaining enlightenment.

Devotion or veneration towards buddhas, bodhisattvas, Buddhist teachings or sacred objects (such as relics) is a common practice among Mahayana Buddhists.

Bowing. The act of bowing (or prostrating) is common throughout Buddhism... Chanting...

Life cycle Rites...

Protective Rites...

Pilgrimage...

Generally, Buddhist teaching views life and death as a continuum, believing that consciousness (the spirit) continues after death and may be reborn. Death can be an opportunity for liberation from the cycle of life, death, and rebirth.

The four noble truths comprise the essence of Buddhas teachings, though they leave much left unexplained. They are the truth of suffering, the truth of the cause of suffering, the truth of end of suffering, and the truth of the path that leads to the end of suffering.

Buddhists believe that the human life is one of suffering, and that meditation, spiritual and physical labor, and good behavior are the ways to achieve enlightenment, or nirvana.

The focus of Buddhist worship is not God, but the Buddha. Any person can be a Buddhist. One does not have to be born into Buddhism, nor do one's parents have to be Buddhists. One can be of any race, country, socioeconomic background, gender etc.

The monks go on alms around in the morning and the only other activities of the day are morning chores, breakfast, and the main meal. Buddhism, the Thai state religion, teaches that use of intoxicants should be avoided.

Specifically, all Buddhist's live by five moral precepts, which prohibit:

The killing of living things...

Taking what is not given...

Sexual misconduct...

Lying...

Using drugs or alcohol...

Buddhist biggest sins are . . .

Killing ones Mother or Father. Slaying an Arhat, slaying a Buddha, and causing division among priesthood.

The tree roots of evil in Buddhism are greed, hatred, and delusion. The inability to see or recognize the

11

truth, particularly the true nature of one's life.

The child spirits are ideally voluntary companions and as such their relationship to the living is based on mutual needs between the living caretakers and the child spirit. The spirits are believed to be waiting rebirth according to Buddhist conceptions of karma and reincarnation.

Haunted by the ghosts of abortion. Thousands of women turn to Buddhist sin-cleansing ceremonies to make amends for terminating pregnancies, but guilt is hard to shift.

Thailand revisits Abortion laws after grim Discovery 2,200 dead fetuses were found in a temple. Monks at the temple deny any blame. Thai

Government crackdown on illegal abortion clinics. Bangkok Post. Abortion is now decriminalized in Thailand thanks to a landmark court case, but access to the service continues to be denied to many women, due to resistance from many medical professionals. The Prime Minister says that the abortion laws are adequate, and no change is needed. Public hospital data reveal that each year approximately 30,000 abortions take place in Thailand, yet most abortions are carried out in private sector facilities, in unmarked abortion clinics, or by self-induction; consequently, 300,000 to 400,000 abortions likely occur each year.

What is a Luk Thep ? or "Child Angels" are plastic life like baby dolls that are believed to be possessed by spirits that bring about good luck and future prosperity. Luk Thep is treated like any other baby or child, they are fed, dressed, and cradled.

Chapter-Three

Escape from Lion City Jail is impossible.

There are two ways out of There:

1. Either in a pine box

2. Or you walk through the front door.

Terry thought that compared to Lion City Prison, going to Thailand would be a walk in the park. He remembered an expatriate called Pat Carr. He got mixed up with a Thai woman. He borrowed money from all over town to supply what his Thai woman could earn outside. She told him that if he wanted to keep her, he would have to pay her what she could earn on the streets.

That was at least s$1,000 per day. (£450)

4th July 2023   Turkey Holiday

It was an all-inclusive holiday, so everything was free. Terry and Belinda went exploring around the Island. Terry brought himself a Hugo Boss belt for 650 Turkish Lira. That's about £21.00 plus several pairs of shorts. They enjoyed sunset walking on the beach. The place was really tranquil, and the food was five stars.

Terry raised a question; you don't mind if I go to Thailand, do you? She replied, 'If you get up to any naughty tricks, I don't want to know, so don't tell me, ok?' Terry was happy with that and said, 'no problem. Belinda, I'm only there for one week, ok?'

5th July 2023

Went to town, walked up and down the Souks Markets. Bought some Nikki shorts.

How big is the lion now?

Went to the Harbor to eat fish. We ate fish, sea bass and mussels with calamari. Got back to hotel at 4pm. Went to pool for a swim. Got pissed on cocktails. Liked Pina Colada, Blue Lagoons, Gin and Tonics, Tequilla Sunrise etc., etc. Went back to the hotel room and had a cat nap then a shower. Ha! Ha! How big is the Lion now!

Belinda said that she had a lovely time in the town, and it was a memory for her that day. Terry hadn't felt this relaxed in a long time. He liked Belinda and she made him feel relaxed. Terry got involved in a haggling match with a trader and beat him down L10.00.00 for his Nikki Hat.

The restaurant was right at the front of the docks. The view of the cruise ships on the harbor was spectacular.

Suited and Booted.

Turkey, Izmir for a week, heaven. Tui resort was gorgeous. Clean, and plenty to do. The food on the other hand was dreadful. Yesterday's leftovers, soured yoghurt that had been replaced with fresh stuff plonked on yoghurt that had gone very warm and rancid. Stale bread and not croissants that looked the part but bread and not pastry. Who were they kidding.

There were plenty of dishes untouched, avoided by the other guests.

The restaurant was immaculate. The staff, brilliant, and so wanting to please if in need.

The night before, we booked up the fish restaurant, as we could only go there once. I dressed up in a long orange, yellow ochre, and brownish, black evening dress. Terry dressed in a suit, light blue shirt, a rich mid blue tie with tiny white, dark blue spotted and his new boss belt bought from Kusadasi town on our first shopping trip a couple of days ago.

He turned around fully booted and suited. His black shiny laced up shoes. His matching jacket and trousers. I walked quietly behind him and kept my distance then admired every inch of him in awe. He looked gorgeous. He turned around and my view was of an adorable man I had never seen before. He excelled with sexiness with his sun tanned, rich glazed, mid blue eyes that gazed into mine. He was gorgeous. I could not stop looking at him. The difference gave him another side to him that I adore.

The food was rubbish but the atmosphere between us was a full-blown memory that I will never forget.

6th July

Terry often wondered what Belinda thought of the fact Terry was an ex-con and what she felt about him and his past 20years at the Lion City Prison. Here is what she wrote.

I met Terry at the train station in Nuneaton for the first time. My daughter took me, mainly for security now knowing what kind of man was going to be my first date. I saw some people come out of the station, but none looked a bit like I envisaged. I got out of the car and walked over to the entrance. A tall man dressed in black was standing to the left of the station. I thought, could it be Terry? He looked as if he were dressed in Ninja attire and tall.

I asked, he turned around and smiled then said, 'you must be Belinda?' I smiled and replied, 'yes, we can walk to the town from here. Shall we?'

We discussed where to sit and have a chat.

He was handsome. There was something about him I found intriguing. He spoke with a beautiful deep, clear neutral accent that melted me. I kept him talking just to hear it over and over again. He was very sincere in everything he said. We got on so well. The day stood still for us to get to know each other a little. I could not wait to see him again. I had never met a man like him before. A wholesome, wellmannered conversationalist with a vast array of depth to his personality. I felt we talked for hours in the local cafeteria in Nunny town. I asked him in one of our conversations when we first spoke what his name was. He told me, Terry Smith. I thought Smith was weird but also thought it could be. Terry had to get back to the station and so we walked together and then waited for the train. He told me he would show me his driving license in conversation and true to his word he did. I was not bothered at the time, but Terry insisted. It never clicked his name was different to what he told me. All I wanted to know was, did he want to see me again. I certainly did. I could have listened and talked to him for hours. He was so interesting and so different.

We said our goodbyes and kissed. I was so nervous. We decided to see each other again.

My daughter picked me up from the station.

When I got home, I could not stop thinking about him, what we talked about and how we were together. I remembered him telling me about his name and to look it up. I never thought anything of it. After an hour or so I thought let's look it up and see what he's on about. On the internet I typed in Terry Johnson and low and behold, there was loads to read and a picture of him years earlier. He was a very young handsome, proud man that had been honored by recognition of sale personality in the newspapers.

I read another memorable piece that read about some murders that had taken place in Lion City Sling and Terry was the guilty person, who did it. I was horrified, traumatized. As I read on, the story line felt like I was reading a crime but grossly exaggerated and due to foreign mind sets, much may have been fabricated. After reading, I still meandered into truth, lie or exaggeration of the real-life events that needed to be told. I told my daughter to read it and she said not to see him again and that I would be putting myself in danger and that I was too precious to take those kinds of risks with my life.

I phoned him. He asked straight away. What did I think. I told him shock, horror, disbelief and surreal. At the same time, I found his honesty remarkable and brave. I applauded his strength and told him I wanted another date. So did he.

Thailand

I'm worried about Terry going to Thailand due to the Mafia and street crime that's rampant. Also, his intent on finding out about baby spirits. It's a moneymaking Buddhist element that could be dangerous due to the people involved wanting to keep that part of their religion quiet and bountiful. The evation of the truth and anonymous to the world.

For Terry there will be danger at every corner from the Buddhist communities. The families that thrive from the shear death of babies taken from the womb prematurely to women wanting abortions for a variety of reasons. It is wrong that any unborn child is forced to death in any way.

Money made and baby spirits tortured to death into the spirit world at all. Terry is putting his life on the line to open the doors to this deceptive organization and very cruelly private world that needs to be told. Terry knew that he was now hunting down the Blacker side of Buddhism.

Terry thought compared to Lion City Prison, going to Thailand would be a walk in the park.

Chapter-Four

Seven a.m., Heathrow airport was already overly crowded on Fridays with every nationality going somewhere. The new airport was a massive infer-structure with hundreds of shops selling their duty-free wears. Terry bought a book from a wellknown book stall and a bottle of Captain Morgan.

It was now eleven a. m. and his flight was due to leave at twelve thirty a.m. Thai airways. All was on schedule. He would not miss this flight. After a twelve hours of a long tedious flight, Terry arrived in Bangkok Airport, Thailand. He had a limousine awaiting for him which took him to his hotel. It was more three-star Hotel. Terry was greeted by the area representative. He offered to show him around. Terry told her he was not interested in any side shows as he had frequented Thailand at twenty-five times. She didn't know what to say and said to him, 'do you have any questions for me?'

He said, 'yes June, I do have a question, 'Have you ever heard of the baby spirits in Thailand?'

She looked at him with a frightened expression and said, 'I sorry, I don't. She looked at me with frightened eyes. That night he rested and had an early night.

The next morning he hired a motorcycle.

He set off to see what the locals claim to be the oldest Temple in Thailand; however, the journey was not so simple.

A silver car hit terry broad side and knocked him off, flying through the air off his bike.

Miraculously, he came off lightly with only a few cuts and bruises. Still dazed, a Thia woman came running up to him screaming and shouting in Thai and broken English.

'I call Police, I call police.'

She was shouting and waving her arms about, but Terry calmly ignored her, didn't think about waiting around. So he resaddled his bike (I wonder if this is the baby spirits at work). He thought.

Chapter-Five

Finding the Temple was not easy. Not because it was on a hill side many steps into the sky. Even a blind man could find. And that was because that every car, motor bike, van or truck that passed the Temple had their horns two or three times as they passed the Temple. They say it is for good luck. When He arrived at the Temple gates and like all the other visitors, he respectfully removed his shoes as a mark of respect.

Next he was greeted by a monk. Behind him was standing behind him was a hundred deities.

The next thing he saw was a table full of fruit on it.

This was before he realised it was an altar. He was then approached by a man and a woman offering a packet of josh-sticks. Of course he had to donate to the slit at the top of the box, which he obliged. Then he was shown around by a monk. All the station of the different deities, the monkey god, the elephant god, the tiger, the dog. Many of these he saw.

At each station he was directed to put three burning candles at the foot of each of the deities.

Terry approached the two monks and was about to ask them a question approached, but both monks shook their heads and replied, 'no speak English. Terry couldn't take anymore of blasting of the horns that each vehicle past by the roadside of the Temple below.

After putting his shoes back on, Terry left for town. Then, he came upon another Temple. This one was much bigger than the other one. And unlike the other one this had a name. WatSuwen Khim Wong Temple.

He came upon two Monks that was sitting around doing nothing. Terry asked their names. The tallest one said, 'Akka Thumo. The second monk

Didn't answer. They were both young monks age about 23 to 30 with bald heads and dressed in their orange robes. Then the second Monk called Sumteto and asked Terry what he was looking for in our Temple. Terry explained to both Monks that he was doing a survey (to disguise Terry writing this book about baby Spirits).

Terry asked them directly, 'what do you know about the baby spirits in Thailand?'

Both Monks looked at each other and shrugged their shoulders. 'What you look for sir' is forbidden for us to talk about it. Terry was persistent, saying, 'please tell me what's it all about, I come a long way to find out about this subject, of why the practice of the giving of baby spirit fetuses at late pregnancies?

Both Monks looked at each other again, then looked at Terry.

Monk Akka Thumo, 'looked at Terry, then said, What you seek is the Kuman Thong (pronounced Ku-man-Thong).

Then second Monk gave his name as Sumetora' said, 'Thai people have beliefs. The band is made of children who died before their birth. Their soul,

'Thai- people believe that they have not gone anywhere.'

Kuman Thong is made up by the witch doctor. These beings are worshipped to obey the beholder, The Kuman Thong protect shippers, for personal gains, protection, wealth, and harm. In some cases it is believed to have consequences to each request.

Kuman Thong is not used in mainstream Buddhism. Kuman Thong has been in Thai society for hundreds of years. There is also a belief that having Kuman Thong will bring good luck.

Then Terry asked another question, 'how do you get the baby spirits. At first neither would say anything. Then the first Monk offered by saying, 'You must go to the witch Doctor first. Then the second Monk interrupted, 'you must pay him for acquiring to get a baby spirit. Adding this practice are forcing the woman to give birth and doesn't happen every day.'

Once more, you can buy one of the witch Doctors on the internet. Then the first Monk added that Kuman Thong said this practice is illegal in Thailand. Kuman Thong is illegal in Thailand. Then Terry asked, 'is there a Witch Doctor in Phuket?'

'But I do know that the witch Doctor will charge you $10,000 Baht.(£238.00) life is cheap in Thailand.'

Then the first Monk said, 'I know a temple baby spirits.'

'Which ones that,' said Terry.

The Monk on Terry's note paper. It was called the,' Wat nat hang nok A yotthya Temple.

Terry googled the name and the voice said, 'why do you want to access this sight?'

The first Monk said, 'you are the public. The general public does not know and the people that do not know about it, will not disclose any information. It's only something the teacher Monk would only disclose the information a junior Monk.'

This information is strictly for Monks only. But, if the teacher would do Kuman Thong may come and hurt us.

That's the reason we can't tell you anymore.

The first Monk says, 'but they are teachers, and it works but very few.' The two Monks stood up and turned around and said, 'that's all we can tell you.' Then turned around and they left the scene. One Monk came back with some orange juice and said, 'good look with your search, 'then walked away. He then added to Terry's search Wikipedia. Terry thought they do fill baby fetuses and that the practice is illegal in Thailand. Next step was to find a Witch Doctor in Phuket. The site also said that baby dolls had baby fetuses inside their body shells.

Historically, lucky symbols and items have been a large part of Thailand traditions. Similar to luck there Luk doll Kuman Thong, which were once made from still born babies. Our figurines that if treated well, would bring good luck to their owners.

The Kuman Thong is in the legend Khum Chang Phaen, where the character Khun- Theon, made one by removing the still born baby from the stomach of his wife, whom he had killed.

Terry was called up to the Hotel reception to be told a man with his passport was waiting for him. When he arrived he found out it was the bike hiring man come to take me to the police station due to the previous accident being reported and that Terry had hit the woman's car with his bike. He was asked to report to the police station at 2 p.m. Which he did.

However, when he arrived at the station there was nobody there.

He was asked to turn up at the station the next day. After arriving at the allotted hour of 2.00 pm the next day he was greeted by the same middle aged ugly woman who had crashed into his bike and screamed at him. Terry remembered she looked like a pig with her nose. Thick and wobbly joules that looked like a pig with a trout nose that deliberately ran into him simply for the money. She was also armed with an Insurance assessor. She was claiming "12,000baht for the damage to her car. Plus her $8'000 compensation for having to be off work. It cost another (£900.00)Eng.

The Thai Police said that this was a civil offence and not a Police matter or a criminal offence.

So you can pay the $18,000 now and that is the end of the matter, or you can go to court to argue your case there. Terry decided to simply put his hands up. He asked where the nearest ATM was to draw the money out just to be able to get home, even though he was not guilty. He wondered what would have happened if he was a poorer tourist unable to fork out a couple of grand just like that for an accident.

Chapter-Six

After all the hassles and the motorbike scene he decided to go all around on the Island to change his scenery and get a breath of fresh air.

He stopped at the beautiful Karon Beach and Kamala Beaches. He saw people surfing and sunbathing. He decided to take the day off to have a day on the beach and still find time for witch hunting.

To take investigation any further, he had to go and visit a Witch doctor. Wat Na Tang Nok Temple. It was a thirteen-hour drive according to google maps. So Terry decided not to take the long trip north but to see what more he could find out locally in the problems of Phuket, as there was plenty to find out. In the meantime he decided to check out the poolside beauties which were totally out of bounds. He made a promise to Belinda that he would be celibate during his Thailand stay.

20th July, Only three days to go before he joins Belinda.

The blacker side of Buddhism had been proven by the admission of the two monks that he visited.

Embarrassed as they were, they had to admit that they were by their own volition that they were a part of the blacker Side of Buddhism.

They also admitted that they were not proud of it, although it happened all the time. After all this had been going on for hundreds of years, why would it stop now.

Terry was frustrated because he could not get any more information. With Belinda's permission, Terry went to a nightclub and scored with a very pretty, commonly called lady boys named Kyle. She was very tall and wore high heels. She had a beautiful smile. I told her immediately, 'I don't want sex, I just want information.' She said, 'what information?'

Terry said,' what do you know about the baby spirits?'

She said, 'I don't know. I want to go to the UK. I don't have a boyfriend. Why do you want my story to be told? I don't care about having a relationship.'

Would you be my friend for some questions.

She had a tattoo on her back.

'Will you give me a massage.

Terry categorically said, 'she undressed and asked for a massage.

Another late foray till three a.m. Terry showed her the door and she obliged.

Terry went back to work the next day. He went to the first temple to get more information, only this time he met a very old Monk. He was old and stooped in his body. His cane that supported his gait was used by his right hand which kept him upright. He was also dressed up in the Monks Orange Gabe. He also had a bald head.

Terry parked his bike and approached the old man. 'Hello. Can you help me please. I am researching my book on Buddhism. Can you please tell me about the Kuman Thong, (Baby Spirits). The old Monk with a withered look had a kind of approachable face. 'Sit down sir(with a well-lined face). I heard about you sniffing around here the other day for information, and I do know what you are looking for. Terry said, 'what is your name to the old man.' I'fl told you that, I would not be able to tell you about Kuman Thong.' They old man carried on, 'well Sir Kuman Thong origination is in necromancy. (Talking to the dead).They were obtained from the desiccated fetuses of children who had died, while still in their mother's womb. The witch doctors are said to have the power to invoke the still born babies to adopt them as their children and use them in their endeavors.

Terry asked a question to the old nameless Monk by saying, 'How do they know that the babies are still born before it is even born?' The old man burrowed his brow and said, 'according to the ancient manuscripts, used by practitioners of black magic, first, young man, the unborn fetus was surgically removed from the mother's womb then the body of the child is taken to cemetery for the conduction of the proper ceremonial ritual to invoke a Kuman Thong. The body was roasted until dry, whilst the witch Doctor chanted incantations of magical script. Once the rite had been completed the dry roast Kuman Thong, and then pasted yalak (a kind of lacquer)using plus amulets and Tak rut with gold leaf. Thus the effigy received the name Kuman Thong meaning golden little gold.

Terry could hardly keep up writing at the same speed as the old Monk's pace.

He continued, 'Some Kuman effigies were soaked innammanphrai a kind of oil extracted by burning a candle close to the chin of a dead child or a person in a violent death or an unnatural death. Or a natural death. This is much less common now. Because this practice is now illegal. Using fat from human babies for the consecrating oil. Occasionally, there are still some amulets obtained through authentic methods appearing in the market. Some years ago a famous Monk was expelled from the Buddhist Sangha for roasting babies. He was convicted. But later continued to make magic as a lay person after his release.'

'Thai all sounds very interesting,' to the old Monk. The old monk, well he said there, 'skumannee. In the case of a female's spirit. The efficacy is not called Kuman Thong but Kuman Nee. Kuma nan

Thong is mentioned in the Thai legend of Khun Chang Khun Phaen, where the character Khun, Phaen, made one by moving the still born baby from the stomach of his wife and killing her.

Terry listened to the old man. 'I am not proud of this side of our Buddhism. It's not like it used to be, He said.

The old Monk got into full swing saying. 'Kuman Thong refers to the spirits of dead babies living in amulets of statues. When you hold the amulet or the statue, you may feel the power of the spirit. Those spirits are not evil spirits. Some of these children die from sickness or accidence and abortion. The spirits of these children cannot be reborn after birth, so they wander around. The Monks here in Thailand want to help the spirits of the children to get a better rebirth. The only way is to admonish them to do good deeds and gain merits for a better life. The monks in Thailand will make the amulets and statues from the reused from the cemeteries soil.

They will chant to guide the spirits into the amulets or statues. They will admonish the children's spirits to do good and protect their owners and keep them from harm.'

Terry asked the old Monk, 'what if the owners of these Kuman Thong amulets have evil intentions?'

'Well said, 'the old Monk. Scratching his chin.

'In these cases both the owners and the Kuman Thong will have bad karma due to them. The owners will suffer more.'
'Is that all you have to tell me sir,' asked Terry. 'As long as you remember,' the old

Monk added, 'that the legend of Kuman Thong has its origins in necromancy and black magic it is illegal. It said that witch doctors will invoke special powers into stillborn children, to grant the mother luck. However, the practice became widespread and profitable. Many witch doctors began performing forced abortions upon the mothers to extract the child, to the point the legend has changed in some parts of Buddhism religious groups to reflect claiming a forcibly removed child is the only way to complete the ritual.

More sins, they influence Kuman Thong to do bad things for them.

They even have stores on the internet selling Amulets online, Saying Thailand Amulets. Thai Buddhists Amulets from Thailand's greatest Monks and lay masters for sale.'

Terry tried to offer the old Monk Money for his troubles, but the old Monk quietly declined. The old man began to shuffle his feet. It was time for lunch. Terry thanked the old man and for his openness about Kuman Thong but before parting ways. Terry turned back a little and said, 'may I come back to see you in the future?'

Terry Johnson was well pleased with the result and with himself. He could not believe his luck. Lastly, the Monk did give a word of advice, 'Please don't pursue this line of enquiry any more or you will get yourself into deep trouble, and harm may come to you when you least expect it...'

Chapter-Seven

Terry's Thailand trip had finally come to an end, He knew he would have to return and track down the witch Doctors who make Kuman thong, from baby fetuses by roasting them. As a final goodbye. It was time for Terry to hand in his rented Motorbike. The repair costs $20,000. This together with the ugly woman's car, made a total of $48,000.

He caught the five-a.m. shuttle to Bangkok only to wait for the longdistance aeroplane until three o'clock in the afternoon. However, he got what he had come for. He found out better information than he thought he would. For instance, he found out the illegal activities about Kuman Thong and how it was rotten to the core.

But first of all, he had to start with the witch-Doctors. Better luck next time on his next adventure.

But I want to keep my baby. I don't' want to give it up screamed the young girl, sixteen years old who had unwittingly ventured into a witch doctors web. She was paid $1000 u.s.d, to have an aborted baby after eight months of pregnancy. 'You took the money girl, now you must give us your baby fetus. Now it is time you must!' 'I'd rather die than lose my baby, she cried.' Tonight it is the full moon when the Kuman Thong spirits are at their most powerful. You will give us your baby or die with it,' said the witch doctor. We have made all the necessary preparations. Grab her!' The two men grabbed her by the arms and tied her to the bed. Then an enforced abortion was carried out by the witch doctor without any fuss. There was blood everywhere. The girl was dead. The baby was also dead, for the method of removing the fetus, was the cruelest of procedures. Straight in with the knife. It was also the best way to obtain the strongest Kuman Thong Spirit. This happened in a soundproof clinic in the back streets of Bangkok City, Thailand.

Then a door slammed followed by the sound of footsteps of someone running away. 'Stop them, whoever they are, this cannot get out. The two men pursued the footsteps but never caught the intruders. He was gone.

The girl was a nobody just one of the millions of young vulnerable but stupid girls that were available for $1000 dollars each. You could buy a baby fetus never mind about the girl because you could sell the girls fetus Kuman Thong's spirit for $10,000 a massive profit for all of us witch doctors of the Kuman Thong.

At midnight in an old disused warehouse on the outskirts of Bangkok. There was a meeting of witch Doctors about a hundred of them, all dressed in black. All were wearing a face mask, the only thing they had in common was that they all had shaved heads. The main man and two others stood side by side and were orchestrating the meeting. The one in the middle spoke, 'We witch doctors should all stick together and form a cooperative of abortion taking fees and fix the price at $1000 per time.

And no one should undercut the price. Do we all agree on that?'

There was a loud raising of voices all saying, 'I', we agree.' 'That's good,' said the head man on the stage unrecognizable apart from his bald head because he was wearing a face mask. Adding, 'O.K. until the next time we meet next month happy abortion taking, at $10,000 a pop we will be rich in no time at all.' The crowd of masked men cheered and laughed saying, 'here, here!' And the gathering of witch doctors broke up for the night.

Chapter -Eight

Klahan meaning "Brave" was sitting in an all-night café drinking strong coffee to keep himself awake. The dead girl's name was Anong, "gorgeous woman" she was a good friend of Klahans. He didn't know who to go to since most of the police force were corrupted. Who could he tell to stop this horrible practice from going on anymore. He was scared. A car drove by slowly while the two occupants viewed the people in the café/bar. He decided to go to the only place he could trust a Buddhist monk at the main temple of Bangkok the Wat Pho temple complex is one of the largest and oldest wats in Bangkok covering an area of 50 rai or 80.000 square meters. He took his shoes off and walked into the complex. It was 4.30 a.m. so he knew that his friend was awake. His Name was Kiet which meant "honor." He met Kiet in the main prayer rooms, gave his friend Klahans a big hug, 'Hi Keit, how are you doing my good friend?' 'I'm fine my friend thanks.' 'What troubles you at this early hour of the morning?' Klahan started to shake again, 'I've just witnessed a murder in the seedy district of the town in Patpong.' He continued in a shaky voice, 'I saw a girl who was heavily pregnant get murdered with a big knife, and at the same time her baby fetus removed from her, it was all one big bloody terrifying mess. So I ran away as fast as I could to here via the café to make sure I wasn't followed.' 'What did you see Klahan?' Asked his friend Kiet. 'I saw three men through the crack of a door in an old warehouse.

59

Two men held the girl tightly while the third held up a big knife. The man with the knife said that he had already invested $1000 eight months ago when he paid for the girls' fetus. Tonight he was collecting on his investment. But the girl named Anong did not want an abortion, in desperation she even offered to pay the main man's $1000 back to him. But she was flatly refused.

So I came here to take some advice from you on what I should do next.' 'Did they recognize you, asked Kiet, did they get a look at your face?' 'No, I don't think so. It was not very well lit up.' 'Still they may have gotten a look at you in pursuit.

'Pack a few things Klahan and get a train out to one of the provinces where it is all quiet and lay low for a while until all is blown over. Then I'll send word for you to come back when it is safe to do so.' 'But where should I go in the provinces ?' 'Go to Wat Suwen Khim Wong Temple in Phuket. I will send word ahead of your arrival, so they will be expecting you. Their names are Monk Akka Thumo and Monk Sumetora, you may confide in them as they are most trustworthy, and they will take good care of you.'

A few days later both monks from the Phuket branch Of the Brotherhood met up with each other.

Over dinner that night they discussed their friend's dilemma They all knew that behind all of this baby fetus snatching was the Kuman Thong witch doctor's movement.

In fact, only the other day, we had a Caucasian here asking us all a about the Kuman Thong. We told him what we could, and we both think he will be back again. What was his name asked Klahan. His Name was Terry, yes that's it, Terry Johnson. I believe he is still in the U.K. I have his email address. Here it is Terry. Johnson58@gmail.com I will send him a message about the most recent goings on around here maybe he could expose them on an international scale.'

The next day Terry Johnson received a message from the Monk Akka Thumo. The message read. Dear Mr Johnson. I trust all is well with you. A number of strange happenings have been going on recently with the witch doctors Kuman Thong movement. We cannot trust our local police force as we believe that they are corrupted. I promised to contact you as you may have some international contacts that could help us in our plight against the Kuman Thong and the witch doctor movement. Especially as the whole of Thailand is now involved. Maybe it would be worthwhile for you to have another visit to Thailand.

Yours Faithfully Akka Thumo.

Terry read the content of the e. mail, thinking this could only be exposed and brought to justice is by the International Criminal Courts of Justice in the Hague.

He talked to Belinda about a second trip to Thailand she said go if you must, it sounds pretty urgent, so yes go!

The following Friday Terry was on TG916 from Heathrow to Bangkok. He caught the connecting flight to Phuket, and checked in the Sea view hotel. He immediately made e-mail contact with Klahan the monk staying at the Wat Suwan Khim Wong temple. They agreed to meet up with the other two monks

Akka Thums and Swumetora, at lunch time that day.

They all met at the Sea view hotel at 1pm in the afternoon. After making formal greetings, Terry was the first to talk, 'so Klahan you were you in Bangkok when you ran into the Witch doctors of the Kuman thong?' 'Yes I think I witnessed a murder of a young girl called Anong.'' How did you know the girl?' Asked Terry. She was a young prostitute who worked the Patpong area of the city. We used to talk together now and again. Only on this night the night of her murder, she wasn't around for our usual chat, but the night before she disappeared she seemed to be a little apprehensive about something. She never told me what. I knew she was seven or eight months pregnant, but she didn't know who the father was.

She was fine with that. She only wanted to keep the baby, that's all.' 'So tell me Klahan, what happened on the night of the murder?' 'Well, like I said, I was due to meet up with Anong for our usual chat about eight p.m. but she didn't turn up, so I walked along her usual route down by the river behind some old disused warehouses. I saw a door open and close, and it wasn't locked so I went in. It was then that I heard the sound of a faint scream of a girl. It was Anong, I'm sure of it. So I followed the sound until I came to some light shining through the crack of a door. I stood there and listened. I heard everything.'

"What did you here,' asked Akka Thumo, leaning forward with interest. 'I could see the outlines of three big men in the room. Two of them held Anong, the girl by the arms and the

65

other, the biggest man of them all did all the talking.' 'What did he say?' asked Terry quizzically?' 'Well there was an argument about money at first something about the girl owing a fetus for a $1000 dollars. Then the girl screamed I want to keep my baby. It's too late said the head man, you've already taken the money eight months ago and now it's time to pay.' 'I'll pay you back your $1000 with interest said the girl.' 'It's too late for any bargain making we'll have your baby's spirit now and your life too if you don't cooperate! shouted the big man. Anong the girl screamed you won't have my baby, never. Pin her down on the bed, Shouted the big man. The other two men did exactly what they were told to do. Then the head man stuck his big knife straight into the woman's belly, shucking her baby out like removing an oyster from its shell.

The girl Anong gave her last scream of help, but it was over. Both mother and baby were now dead; the place was awash with blood and guts.

I must have said something mentioned Klahan, because one of the men turned around and saw that the door was not secure and the he could hear me breathing heavily through the crack of the door. That's when I decided to run for my life. So I ran for at least half an hour before coming to a busy roadside café/bar where I inter mingled with the crowd. I knew they had lost me. So after about an hour or more, I went to seek help and found Kiet at the Wat Pho big Budda temple in the city. He's on our side he was the one who told me to come to Wat Suwen Khim Wong Temple here in Phuket to hide out until it's was over. The trouble is that this practice of taking babies in Thai society has been going on for hundreds of years what's going to put a stop to it now ?' 'We are,' said Terry Johnson,' adding, 'This has to be made publicly known worldwide and the main culprits have to be brought to the International Criminal Courts of Justice at the Hague for punishment.

Klahan said, 'The problem is we are up against ruthless killers and a gang of greedy Witch doctors. They meet once a month usually in an old, disused, warehouses on the outskirts of Bangkok city. That much I managed to find out about while a was in Bangkok.

We have to go to Bangkok. Now. Time is of the essence, 'said Terry Johnson. We'll all go tomorrow. First of all, we will go and see Kiet at the Wat Pho Temple and see what he has to say about what has been going on in Bangkok central. Klahan said 'I'll introduce us all to Monk Keit in Wat Pho. We'll all be safe if we stay at that temple.' So, the next day, Terry Johnson left Phuket with Klahan, Akka Thumo, and Sumetara on an unknown journey full of unknown risk and dangerous witch doctors of the Kuman Thong.

Chapter-Nine

They all arrived safely on the 6 a.m. morning shuttle from Phuket to Bangkok, and quickly made their way across town to the Wat Pho Temple, where all four of them were greeted warmly by senior Monk Kiet. He was a middle-aged monk with big brown eyes, laughter lines on his face, and a freshly shaven head. 'Welcome to Bangkok my friends. You're just in time to join us for breakfast. They all sat down to a meal of rice, fish with vegetables, and flat bread.

After breakfast, for privacy they all decided to meet up in the small prayer room at the back of the temple. Led by

Kiet, followed by Terry, Klahan, Akka Thumo, and Sumetara.

Kiet spoke first, 'welcome to Wat Pho Temple gentlemen. We all know what we are here to do, and that's to expose the Kuman Thong witchcraft gang. First of all we must be aware of the danger that we will be putting ourselves in the firing line as it were of both the Witch doctors and the harmful effects of the Kuman Thong, which can come to harm us from any side and at any time. And the Christian holding of a crucifix in the direction of evil to ward it off, will not work against the eastern religion of the Kuman Thong.

We must first go on what we do know and that is the murder of the girl Anong and her baby fetus.

We start from there. You Klahan, you're the best person to go to on this as you were a first-hand eyewitness of this ghastly affair. Hopefully they didn't recognize you after the fact and also the fact that you got clean away is of great benefit. It was in the district of Phra Nakhon Si Ayutthaya. In the old warehouses in Ban Chang by the lake. That's the lake that I think they are sinking the bodies of the woman in heavy chains. We also know that the Bosses of the Witchcraft Kuman Thong group have a meeting every Friday at the Riverside golf club, that's only a 48-minute drive to the infamous Wat Na Tang Nok Temple. That is the temple where we know you can for a price of up to $10.000 buy your own Kuman Thong baby spirit, from one of the many Witch doctors available, that stay at that temple.'

All five men sat at the table when Terry Johnson made a direction. 'O.k. men, let's all split up and see what we can find out about the Kuman Thong Witch Doctors. But be on your guard remember they already know that someone spotted them in one of the murders last week. Kiet, you stay here and hold the fort. Akka Thumo and you Sumetara, go to Wat Na Tang Nok temple and pose as a potential buyer of a baby spirit Kuman Thong. See what you can get there. Klahan and I will go check out the lake and the old warehouses at Ban Chang in the district of Phra Nakhon Si Ayutthaya. Then we will go and check out the Riverside Golf club that's less than an hour away from Wat Na Thong Nok Temple. We will all meet up back here at 6 p.m. tonight o.k. Has anybody got any questions?' No one raised their hands, and they all went about with their respected tasks.

Akka Thumo and Sumetara went to the Wat Na Thong Nok Temple, took their sandals off their feet, and began to pray, looking like two ordinary Monks doing what monks do, that's pray. Then after praying Sumetara casually asked one of the other monks if he knew where he could buy a top of the range baby spirit? The lay monk replied, 'the best way to get a spirit is to go to the High witch doctor monk called Channarong "experienced warrior." He is very busy all the time, so you'll have to make an appointment to see him.' 'How do I make an appointment to see the witch doctor Channarong?' 'You must go through his secretary. His name is Sakda "dominance" Sumetara, find out where to go and get an appointment. He approached the monk Sakda and ask if it were possible to make an appointment to see the witch doctor Channarong to get a baby spirit. Sakda is a round solid Monk, built like a sumo wrestler with fat cheeks and short stubby fingers, weighing at least 140kg. Held an appointments book in one hand a pen in the other, said In a growling low voice, 'What is your business here?'

'I have come to see the mighty one, Monk Channarong,' adding differently, 'to see if I can acquire a Kuman Thong baby spirit.

Sakda replied in a haughty manner, 'they are now $10.000 each you know, can you afford it monk? 'It's monk Sumetora from the Phuket lodge Sir. Well I haven't got much time my boy!' Quickly thinking on his feet Sumetora said, 'I can afford it. I have a wealthy client, a white man from Briton wants one for him and one for his wife.' 'That would be $20,000 U.S. for the two.' 'Yes, 'replied Sumetora. 'that's right 20 k for two.'

'O.K Sakda. I will consult the great one, and see if Monk, Channarong is available for your request he will see you about a month from now don't come empty handed bring your white man and his money, at 12 midnight on the next full moon that's three weeks from now.' 'Fine, we'll be here, 'said monk Sumetora, shaking under his robe. Thinking to what evil he had committed himself and Terry Johnson too.

He met up with Akka Thumo outside still shaking with fear after meeting up with one of the evilest men he had ever met. And he was only the secretary for Monk and witch doctor Channarong that he and Terry Johnson would have to meet in a Months' time, if not before. They both headed back to base temple Wat Pho to meet up with the others at six as planned.

Terry Johnson and Klahan turned up at the old warehouses at Ban Chang by the lake. This was in the district of Phra Nakhon Si Ayutthaya. There was a about a dozen old warehouses stuck together beside a large lake. After exploring around the lake for any sign of anything untoward. They'd need scuba diving gear to explore the depths of the lakebed. Both men approached the old disused warehouses to see what they could find. They opened the old creaky door only to find it dark inside. Only seeing dimly, they followed each other to the place where Klahan had witnessed the gruesome murder of the young girl Anong and her unborn. They came to the spot where Klahan stood and watched the murder, but all was spotless no bloodstains anywhere everything had been cleaned up. Terry looked at Klahan and asked him in a quizzical tone, 'Are you sure this was the place where you saw the girl being murdered?' 'Yes Terry my friend, this is exactly where it happened, and they've done a bloody good job of cleaning things up.' 'Let's go to the riverside golf course, its Friday at noon the organization of witch doctors and Kuman Thong meet there every Friday for lunch.

They arrived at the Riverside Golf club not far away from the lake and warehouses. They were ushered into the main bar and billiards room just off the dining room with its view over the 18ᵗʰ hole. They were both immediately recognized as being nonmembers of the club. 'If you want a drink sir as non-members, you'll have to be signed in by a member of the club said the usher.' 'That's O.K. I'll sign them in shouted a stranger a small man with a pot belly and a smiling face. My name is Decha "Brave". I am the secretary of the clubhouse, so the drinks are on me, Adding, we are always on the lookout for new members of the club, and you are?' Terry introduced himself and his partner Klahan. They both ordered a lime juice. 'I can show you around the club if you like,' said Decha smiling. They both agreed. 'Before we go, can I ask you a question?' said Terry. 'Certainly said Decha. Go ahead ask away!' shouted the club secretary. 'What do you know about the Kuman

Thong and its organization of baby spirits? '

'You're not police are you? 'said the secretary. 'No we are not the police sir, only private individuals, looking for some answers.'

'Answers to what,' said Decha.' 'Well very recently and not too far away from here there was a murder of a young girl called Anong and her baby fetus.'

'A murder you say. No I know nothing of a murder of a girl and her baby, oh no, not around here.' I'd show you around the rest of the place but the dining room is fully booked by our very own Kuman Thong witch doctors they book out the whole dining room every Friday. It's a private meeting room or I would admit you in there,' said Decha.

'Who's chairing the meeting?'

'Channarong(experienced warrior), our leader,' said Decha.

'I'd like to ask Mr Channarong a few questions of my own.'

'The meeting room is booked all day I'm afraid I can't let you just wander in there unannounced.'

'Well announce me then as Terry Johnson and Mr. Klahan. Representing Human Rights commission of the Hague universal criminal justice courts.

Chapter-Ten

Terry, together with Klahan, raced to open the double doors of the meeting room. Inside there was about 200 bald men all sitting facing the front of the podium where a man stood there addressing his audience. He was Huge over seven feet high and broad shoulders. He was huge with a round head, big black eyes, clean shaven and a Hitler style mustache on his top lip. All his Audience turned around to look at the two intruders. When suddenly there was a booming voice that echoed around the room. 'What is the meaning of this rude interruption?'

'I'll tell you,' shouted back Terry Johnson. 'We are here representing the Human rights movement, of the Hague world-wide criminal courts of justice. Last week a girl and her baby fetus was murdered By the so-called Kuman Thong baby spirits gang of witch doctors. We believe that the perpetrators are in this very room, and we mean to catch them. We also believe that many other girls are being killed every month just for their baby fetuses.'

'Nonsense!,' shouted Channarong.

'Very soon we'll be able to prove it,' shouted Terry back.

'And what makes you think that Mr. Johnson? I have my sources of this practice does exist among your followers. That you are buying baby fetuses at $US 1000 and selling the same baby fetuses for $U.S 10.000 per fetus. And I aim to prove it beyond any reasonable doubt that this is going on, on a regular basis.'

'Guards throw them out of here now!'

Four guards tried to grab Terry and Klahan by the arms and remove them, but they were too strong for them. So Terry shouted out to Channarong, 'We know the way out and we'll be back with the proof.'

Where upon the meeting broke up and all the bald-headed participants went home.

'Let's head back to Wat Pho Temple and meet up with the others at 6pm. At least we've rattled their cages, 'said Terry to Klahan. AkkaThumo, Sumetora and Kiet were already in the small prayer meeting room waiting for them to return.

Once they had all sat down Terry took the Chair, 'O.K. everybody what have we all learned or picked up today?' 'Sumetora.' 'Well I've booked an appointment with Terry Johnson to go to the Wat Na Tang Nok Temple on the pretense of buying two baby fetuses in the form of Kuman Thong. But I can't do it now because Terry has already got together with Channarong at the Golf course meeting. So he would recognize him immediately,' 'I'll go in his place,' said Kiet adding, 'I haven't done anything yet!,' 'in an exited tone. Ok what's the deal with the purchase of the Kuman Thongs?' Said Terry. 'Well, said Sumetora adding, I met up with one huge man named Sakda. He said that if I wanted to purchase two baby sprits I would have to bring the buyer plus $20.000 in cash. Next month at 12 midnight on the full moon and obtain two Kuman Thongs. I'd have to go through the whole baby spirit ceremony. And I suppose we'd also have to witness the murder of two pregnant girls.

That gives us four weeks to set something up and expose the scam for what it is.'

Kiet spoke up.

'I have a very pretty girlfriend in Bangkok her name is Urassaya, "Queen of Beauty." She's very intelligent and knows all about the Kuman Thong and hates the way they do business. I talked to her last week she was only too willing to lend a hand and she's also willing to pretend that she is six or seven months pregnant. She can do that by wearing a special prop over her stomach. She also knows that it's dangerous to mess around with the Kuman Thong. She's ideal for what we want.' 'When can we meet her,' Asked Terry. 'Today if you like, 'Replied Kiet. 'Great lets set up a meeting with Urassaya first thing tomorrow morning here at the temple,' Finished Terry.

Chapter-Eleven

It was nine a.m. on a smoggy 30c Monday morning, in Bangkok.

All six participants of the clan of Kuman Thong busters were present. At the Wat Pho Temple Bangkok, there was a small prayer room. Terry Johnson presumed leader, started at the meeting. 'Thank you for attending this meeting of minds. I would like to introduce a new member to our clan, and she is 29 year old, works in the media sector. Her name is Urassaya.'

Urassaya a very attractive girl and at 1.75 meters was tall for an Asian lady. With beautiful hazel brown eyes. Perfectly shaped lips. She spoke out for the first time and said she, like us, hated the way The Kuman Thong and the Blacker side of Buddhism works. So she's prepared to go to any lengths to bring down these murders of young girls and their even younger fetuses.

'Well let's get down to business shall we. Urassaya I'd like to see how convincing you look dressed up, as a pregnant woman. Because Kiet is going to be your pimp and sell your baby fetus to the Kuman Thong for $1000 today so go get yourself changed, 'O.K., 'She said. And off she went.

Akka Thumo and Sumetora, the two monks from Phuket. 'I want you to do some canvassing in the blue light district of Patpong 1 and Patpong 2, I want you to interview as many whores as you can and ask them if they have ever been asked to sell their fetuses for $1000 by the Kuman Thong. And also is there anybody out there who is expecting a baby and who is looking to abort their pregnancies for money. The more information you can glean the better for our cause. See you back here at six.' So off went Akka Thumo and Sumetora together to the redlight prostitute's district.

Kiet brought Urassaya back to the temple fully clad in disguise as a seven - or eight-month pregnant woman of the streets of Bangkok. 'Well what do you think?' Asked Urassaya giving her long black platted hair a little twirl.

'Perfect,' said Terry and agreeing, 'Yes,' said Klahan. Adding, 'You look great.' 'Now all you have to do is stand on the street corners and look for some sexual favors to help you out with the cost of having a late pregnancy, terminated.

Off you go then see you back here at six.
'O.K?' And off they went. That left Terry
Johnson and Klahan with something to
do. We could always hire some scuba
diving gear and go check out the bottom
of the lake at Ban Chang in the district
of Phra Nakon Si Ayutthaya. 'OK, let's
go and do that. The weather is fine and
sunny we should have great visibility
at 50 meters,' said Terry. So, off they
went. Now the whole team were busy
with their individual tasks of the day.
They would be no letup, they would
continue to harass the Kuman Thongs
mission of precuring young girls, for
their fetuses until they got sick of them
continuingly disturbing their business.
This was deadly serious from now on
they were playing for keeps.

On the same day at the Wat Na Thong
Nok Temple the headquarters of the

Witch doctor Kuman thong, there was a meeting going on in the large prayer room. Present were the President, seven feet high Channarong sporting his Hitler copy mustache, with his dark black eyes, thin lips, and sharp teeth. Also present was his secretary Sakda and Decha, the Golf club house manager. And a new rarely seen or invited member of the clan going by the name of Anurak "Heavenly" he was the groups hit man. Although only five foot 8 inches. He was a man of ill repute, a nasty man to know, and even worse to encounter as an enemy. He was a very good sniper at 500 meters as he was in close bodily combat. He was menacing to look at. His face was pock marked with many acne scars from when he was young he had a long scar on the left-hand side of his cheek that started at the eye line and went down to the tip of his chin.

So the four of the evilest men in Southeast Asia were in the one room together. Starting the meeting was the boss of them all Mr Channarong he said loudly almost shouting, 'Okay men, These are my orders. You are going to eliminate all opposition to our witch doctor Kuman Thong business. You will begin with the elimination of this Mr. Terry Johnson and his small gang of miscreants. I want them all dead before the next full moon meeting of the witches Kuman Thong meeting.' 'But we only know Mr Terry Johnson. We don't know the rest of them or even how many they have.' Exclaimed Sakda the group's secretary. 'Then find out how many there are put the word out on the street. Round up the usual suspects, you will find, and eliminate them for sure. 'I need photographs so that I have legitimate targets to aim at,' said Anurak the hit man. Then Decha interrupted, 'I have seen two of them at the golf club. I would definitely remember what they looked like if I saw them again.' 'You'll see them again alright, dead that's when you'll see them growled Channarong, the boss,' adding, 'I want a full report about this mob by tomorrow.'

Sakda, Decha, Anurak all agreed with their boss's request and got their men out on the streets to look for Terry Johnson's small gang of six. These being Klahan, Akka Thumo, Sumetora, Kiet and lastly the beautiful but pregnant looking,

Urassaya. All of them were currently very busy with their daily chores of how to bring down the Blacker side of Buddhism.

Chapter-Twelve

Terry and Klahan went to Dive supply at Ratchathewi. They hired enough air tanks to last them the whole day. They thought they'd try their luck at Nong Bon Lake Park Near Prawet. In the district of Samut Prakan. They hired a boat from the Nong Bon water sports center. And began their dive in grid formation across the lake which was fifty meters deep in parts. Deep enough to hid the weighted down bodies. Hiring a local spotter They both went down at the same time.

They didn't have to dive for very long when they discovered hundreds of female bodies all tied up and weighted down with thick iron chains. Alas it was a horrible spectacle to behold. All in different stages of decomposition their long black hair slowly waving to and frow in the currents as they floated by the ghastly scene. It was like something out of a horror movie. From the different stages of the rotting corpses it looked like this had gone on for some time maybe years and not just months. An hour later they resurfaced again but didn't tell their spotter anything. Who could they tell. Certainly not the local police. They had to tell the international police of the Hague, and report that they had come across over 500 bodies or more of female corpses on the bottom of Lake Nong Bon Lake park. They had to find out if they could make contact with someone in the European side of the international police force. Either in

The Hague or London, Paris, Greece, or even Spain. He had to get the European side involved this would give him more power to make the arrests that were required by the authorities of International Law. Satisfied with what their day had accomplished they set off back to their little H.Q. at Wat Pho Temple. It was nearly six o'clock time to report to their colleagues and report their ghastly and grizzly findings at lake Non-Bong Park.

Akka Thumo and Sumetora had been canvassing all day long in the redlight districts of Bangkok. Thet started out from the Mariamman Temple and from there they slowly walked down Pan road then onto Silmom road, then down to Silom 15 Alley. It was here where they met their first prospective prostitute she was wearing a mini skirt and a low-cut top showing her bosom. Her face was thick with make-up and her hair was all greasy and lank. If you looked carefully at her body you could see that she had a lump on her stomach. Yes she was pregnant. Akka Thumo asked her a question 'What is your name girl?' The girl replied, 'Sherine is my name why do you ask.?' Akka Thumo asked if she was pregnant, and if so how many months? The girl replied, 'I am only a few months pregnant, and I will take both you and your friend for two thousand baht each if you wish. I have a place nearby we can go to.' 'No thank you,' said Akka Thumo politely. He only wanted information. 'What information is that?' 'Has anybody come to you and offered you any money for your baby fetus inside you?' 'Funny you should say that but just the other day a man from The Kuman Thong came to me and offered me $1000 dollars for my baby before it was born. I thought it funny that he should want the baby before it was due only seven or eight months old.' 'Did you take the money Sherine?' said Akka Thumo. 'Why yes as a matter of fact, yes I took his money, He said he would be back this way for me to take me to a place where I would be operated on and have my baby removed. I thought it was all a bit strange but for a $1000 dollars who wouldn't do it, I don't want the baby anyway.' 'When exactly did he say that he would be back to take you to remove your baby?' Asked Sumetora. 'Five weeks from now on 21ˢᵗ of August.'

'Do you want to keep your baby?' asked Sumetora. 'I don't know when I was only a few months pregnant I wanted to have an abortion but now I'm not so sure.'

'We will come back on the 21st of August and confront this man who wants your baby ok Sherine.' 'Oh that would be so kind of you if you would help me save my baby.' They left the girl to go about her business of prostitution and walked down Pramuan road and had a coffee in the Kaze coffee shop, a top-rated place and the two monks were made to feel welcome. In there they could see through the crowded, smoky room that they were a least a dozen Whores looking out for business. The two monks Akka Thumo and Sumetora split up and started asking the girls questions about their businesses and if they'd had any offers for their unborn fetuses. By the end of the afternoon they had accumulated about a dozen girls each who had confirmed dates that they would be collected from this up-market coffee shop, to have their abortions done and that they would be returned safely on the same day that they were taken for surgery. That date was the same day as the first girl Serine, yes the 21st of August. The Monks made a note of this and seeing that the time was drawing near to six o'clock. They left the coffee shop in Pramuan Road and headed for the Wat Pho Temple to their little prayer meeting room.

Kiet playing the Pimp for Urassaya, and she dressed up pretending to be seven or eight months pregnant. Spent the day located in the busiest part of town they both started out from the Chalom Pier to the Chalom Roundabout, then to the fish market. Kiet was acting as a Pimp for the lovely, but pregnant Urassaya, he walked behind her approximately five meters so he was close enough to pounce on any trouble makers. She was stopped numerous times by time wasters asking her for the time of day or asking her if she was single and asking her for directions, and dates. Then a welldressed man in his fifties approached her and paid her compliments about her good looks and the fact that he could not but notice that she was well pregnant into her seventh or eight month. He asked her if she was looking forward to having her baby? She replied that she hated the fact that she was pregnant and couldn't afford to have an abortion, and now it was too late. 'Not so he,' said. Saying, 'I know a man who will pay you one $1000 dollars just to have your foetus removed in the next month of your pregnancy. That's when Kiet got the signal from Urassaya she waved her hand through her hair. Kiet quickly descended on the old rich man and hailed, 'What's going on here,' he said. Kiet was a powerful man at six feet three inches with powerful biceps an imposing figure. She introduced Kiet as her brother who was helping find a wealthy man to take care of her and help her with her late abortion. The man said that's no problem he cannot come with you though when you have your late abortion. 'And why not,' said Kiet. 'Well for a start, because of the lateness of the pregnancy, we need to keep the location a secret. But he said you can stay at a secret location close by and wait for her if you like, that's no problem.' 'When do we get paid the grand,' said Kiet. 'I will pay you now and I will come and collect the lovely Urassaya nearer the time of her abortion let's say on the 21st of August. 'That's a month from now.' The Man then pealed of 50 twenty-dollar notes of his big roll of bank notes and put it in Kiet's hand. 'There now, we are all done now all we do is wait until the 21st of August, and I'll come and collect you both from the fish market on off Chalom Pier Road. Say around six p.m. at night.' Then the fat looking rich old man disappeared back into the crowded streets. 'What do you think of that,' asked Urassaya to Kiet. 'I don't know what to say. Look, it's time we should be heading off back to the old Wat Pho Temple and make our report at six o clock. Let's go!'

The big round table at the Wat Pho Temple in the small prayer room was full. With Terry Johnson leading the debrief as was his second in command Klahan. Then Akka Thumo, Sumetora from Phuket, lastly Kiet, and Urassaya from Bangkok, still wearing her pregnant attire.

Well we all have a story to tell about what happened today and we have certainly poked the hornets' nest and got the Witch doctors & Kuman Thong operations attention. Klahan and I went scuba diving today at Nong Bon Lake Park and found what could fill a cemetery full of underwater graves. After listening to you all tonight you have exposed enough evidence to prove that the Kuman Thong witch doctors are alive and doing very well in business, by offering young girls $1000 for their babies which are then sold on to eager waiting buyers for $10.000 a pop. So as far as I have ascertained is that everything is timed to happen on the 21st of August this year, which incidentally, happens to be a full moon. We have got approximately one month to plan, stop and execute. We'll call it

Operation abortion

'Okay folks,' Terry said, adding, 'That's all for now let's reconvene at 8. A.m. here in the morning, to discuss our next move in the game of abortion stopping. Everybody is dismissed good night.

Chapter-Thirteen

All was busy in Channarong's Kuman Thong camp. As the operations work late at night. It made it harder to track them down. Down at the Riverside Golf club things were getting pretty busy. In the meeting room was the leader giant Channarong the boss. Sakda his personal secretary Decha the Golf club manager, and the Fearless Anurak the hit man was also there. All sitting around a long glass top table sipping green tea. It was Sakda who spoke first. "I have found us a warehouse to rent for the big night of the 21st. It's called the "Sermsuk warehouses at 721 Charoen Nakon road. It has over 20.000 square meters of space plenty of room for our needs and its positioned right next door to the river and lake that we use for our disposal work.

'Excellent work Sakda, 'Bellowed Channarong Adding, 'we only need it for the 21st of August. 'When do we move in and start to make it look like a hospital?' 'As soon as next week, 'replied Sakda. 'Very good Sakda Very good!'

'Now Decha how is the golf club doing?' 'Very good thanks to the profits from the underground casino club.' 'Very well Decaha,' Nodded Channarong, 'Very well indeed.'

'Now what about our famous hit man. What have you got planned for the day Anurak?', asked Channarong in a simple plain tone of voice, he had a lot of respect for his hit man. He had been working for him for many years now, so he didn't want to upset him. 'I plan to kill at least one a day from today until they are all niellated. I've been told that they hang around the Big Wat Pho Temple. I shall go there today and track at least one of them down. There will be blood spilt in the Temple that's bad Karma, 'said Decha the Club manager. 'I don't believe in that bullshit Karma tails, 'Replied Anurak, with an ice-cold stare at the manager. Sakda reported that one of his men had found out that they had infiltrated the prostitutes by canvasing them about their pregnancy terminations and asking them not to go ahead with their abortions if they don't want to.

'That's enough!' shouted Channarong. Off you all go do your duties. With that said they all dispersed all over the city like a rash.

That night Akka Thumo and his friend Sumetora from Phuket were taking their evening meal of rice and plain vegetables, when suddenly there was an almighty crash! The table where they were sitting was turned upside down. Plates of food and dishes crashed everywhere. 'What the hell was going on,' shouted the manager of the restaurant. In that instant a long knife came out of nowhere and slashed a gash right across Sumetoras throat from ear to ear right to the bone. Blood gushed out of Sumetoras throat. He gasped for air but there was none to be had. Akka Thumo tried in vain to help his partner by trying to stem the flow of blood coming from his friend's throat but there was too much blood. His friend was bleeding out now. It was all too late. The ambulance arrived. The

Paramedics went to work on Sumetora, but he was gone...

Later his body was removed to the big Temple the Wat Pho, and he was cremated in the traditional way. Terry Johnson called an emergency meeting for the remainder of the gang that being five members in total. They all grieved over the tragic loss of their gang member. Poor Sumetora he didn't have to die this way thought Terry Johnson. But what could he do. He couldn't hide until the 21st of August, he had to do something before then and fast. But what could he do?

Terry said, 'O.K. We now know that the Kuman Thong are armed with knives and most probably guns. In order to protect ourselves we must do the same. We must arm up with long knives and nine-millimeter pistols.' 'Where do we get them from? Any offers?' 'My uncle' said Kiet, 'Is a member to a local Bangkok shooting range in Phahonyothin road in the Phaya Thai District. He can get us guns and knives.' 'O.K., said Terry let's all go over to your uncles gun club and get some guns and while we are there we can practice our shooting talents on both pistol and rifle range.' Adding, 'Who knows one of us may turn out to be a marksman,' Finished Terry.

At the gun club they had fun hitting targets all day long, but Urassaya came out tops with a nine-millimeter pistol. Then Kiet proved himself worthy with the rifle range scoring top marks at both 300 and 500 meters with an automatic assault rifle. They practiced every other day with the guns. On alternate days where used to practice using a knife with a qualified knife fighting instructor. After a couple of weeks they were fully qualified fighters with either knife or guns.

Akka Thumo from the Wat Suwen Khim Wong Temple in Phuket missed his partner a lot. He wanted revenge, and he wanted it now. He could hardly wait to get back at the Kuman Thong to get his revenge.

Terry's gang were now fit and ready for fighting a battle from what ever came at them from the Witch doctors of the Kuman Thong.

Terry ordered his team to take a rest and lay low until he could form another plan of attack on the Kuman Thong. Revenge is like a dish a salad best eaten cold or so the saying goes. He thought.

That night Kiet the tough monk from the Wat Pho Temple in Bangkok was feeling bored and went for a walk in the red-light district. He walked up Sukhumvit road across from the Nana Hotel which was walking distance from the BTS Skytrain's "Nana Station" He walked to Patpong taking in the scene of all the working girls they were trying to drum up business by showing off their bodies and pole dancing wearing only tight bikini briefs. He was now in what is known as the infamous internationally renowned red-light district. Just walking slowly through the crowds minding his own business. Losing himself in the gaiety of the atmosphere. When suddenly out of the crowds stepped two large men waving samurai swords. Then before Kiet could react one of the two men struck at Kiet's arms and hands and with one all mighty clean swipe, he managed to sever both arms off at the elbow. Then there was a scream from the crowd, followed by another. One of the attackers shouted 'Take from us and we'll take from you that's a message from the Kuman Thong to you.' Then just as quickly as he came he ran off in the same direction back though the crowd where he first came from. This left Kiet still in shock, holding out his two stumps of arms where there used to be arms and hands. Blood was spurting out from both arms from his elbow joints; he wandered around aimlessly through the people who were all giving him a wide birth.' Will someone help me please and call an ambulance. Nobody seemed to move, but someone must have called the emergency services. Within minutes there were two paramedics on the scene of horror. They applied a tourniquet on both arms, and this temporarily stopped the bleeding. Then just as quickly they put Kiet and his two severed limbs into the ambulance with him and with lights flashing and sirens blowing they were off to the hospital A&E department, with a bloody armless monk on board.

Back at the Witch doctors Kuman Thong Wat Na Tang Noks Temple.

They had all listened to the report of the Monk losing both his arms at the elbow was very funny indeed.

Contrary to popular belief that monks don't drink. Today they celebrated, and all raised a glass full of strong mead. That's two of theirs done for. One dead with his throat slashed and one armless' what can he do? Exactly' nothing at all, they all laughed and made a joke of it "he is armless 'They all cheered, two down now, and not many more to go? Then we can all resume our normality of relieving young vulnerable girls of their late pregnancies. For only $1000 and get an immediate return of $10.000 that's an instant profit of $9.000 that's 900%, and it's all ours. Clearly they were all in a happy mood as the 21st of August was just around the corner, they could hardly wait.

Chapter-Fourteen

Back at the big Wat Pho Temple in the small prayer room. Every one was in somber mood having lost two of their colleagues. One being Sumetora and one being Kiet with the amputation of both his arms in a side street in Bangkok. On his own turf.

Terry Johnson had reported the crimes to his Greek contact Apollo Papadaki who had good connections with the criminal courts of Justice. He would eventually fly to Athens and report all that happened so far. He also had a contact in Paris Louis Lambert. who also had great connections in the Hague criminal courts. However, he needed more evidence, to prove his case in the Criminal Law courts of the Hague. But today it was time to strike.

They all got together and decided to burn down the whole Wat Na Tang Nok and the golf course club house. Terry went together to the chemical store in Bangkok and found a chemical store in the Bang Kapi District. Terry knew how to improvise and make an I.E.D. bomb out of chemicals. Posing as farmers Klahan did all the talking and soon found the chemicals he wanted to build two bombs needed for their offensive attack on the Kuman Thong.

This was done by mixing Peroxides (inorganic) when mixed with combustible materials, barium, sodium, and potassium form explosives that ignite very easily. Phoe phosphoruse (P), both red and white, forms explosive mixtures with oxidizing agents Terry needed these chemicals to be made into two lots and planted into two trucks to explode. One truck for the Wat Pho Temple, and one for the golf course to be placed outside the club house on a Friday lunch time when it was at its busiest time of the week. (the Witch Doctors would be.) That would be the weekly meetings of the Witch Doctors Kuman thong were taking place. Klahan and the other target would be done at six o'clock in the evening for evening prayer by the Kuman Thong.

Friday had come around and Klahan drove one of the two old trucks they had procured for the job. Akka Thumo drove the other truck to the golf course to ignite at 1.30 p.m. Both trucks were in position and could be detonated by telephoning the bombs to ignite.

1.30 Came around as the first bomb exploded outside the golf club. What an explosion it was. The whole club site was raised to the ground, leaving nothing behind but a huge smoking crater. There were bodies everywhere. Some crying for help other's just wandering around in shock and disbelief. Most of the attendees were vaporized in the initial explosion, but others were not so lucky with 80 degree burns on their bodies they would die very slowly and very painfully. A fleet of Ambulances turned up to the scene to assist the badly burned and the wounded.

Just as everyone was getting themselves together, at the bomb site. The rest of the witch doctors decided to go to pray at their Temple the Wat

Na Thong. That's where the Kuman Thong keep their headquarters. The witch doctors all sat down to pray to their respected gods, the place was packed out with worshipers.

It was 6. 29. Terry Johson and his crew of four were sitting and watching at a safe distance from what was going to be carnage in just 30 seconds time! Then Boom! The explosion came to there ears a second later. There was a flashing light followed by a huge shockwave explosion. The Temple simply blew apart. Shards and debris flew up to several hundred feet in the air. It was truly an amazing scene to watch from a safe distance away.

Within two minutes the whole temple was also raised to the ground. The deaths from both the Golf club and the Wat Na Tang Nok Temple together would have to be up in their thousands.

Terry was very pleased with the results. Thinking allowed <u>You take from us and we'll take from you.</u>

Chapter-Fifteen

All the remaining team members were pleased with the results of both explosions. As they remembered their former colleagues. Urassaya said that she was going to meet Kiet in the Bumrungrad International Hospital where he was recuperating. Terry said to her to be careful because they may have the Hospital covered. 'Ask the police to put an escort on the door to prevent the Kuman Thong from having a second go at Kiet while he was in his Hospital bed.'

When Urassaya got to the hospital reception she asked for the name of her former colleague in arms, and that she was there on a visit. The duty nurse said in Thai that she was very sorry, but Mr. Kiet has been killed by someone posing as a doctor, killed him by injecting air into his veins this sent him into a cardiac arrest, and we lost him at 06.30 this morning. I am so sorry for your loss.

Word was out the infamous Channarong the Kuman Thong leader was also staying at the same hospital and was in a serious but stable condition after the explosion at the golf club lunch. But his room she discovered, was heavily guarded by two men with machine guns. What a missed opportunity.

The good news as far as Terry Johnsons crew were concerned was that the ruthless Decha, the golf club manager had also been killed at the club explosion. He was decapitated by flying debris. So were another 150 witch doctors dead. All killed by the blast of the explosion at the golf club that day.

Terry decided along with the rest of his team those were, himself, Klahan, the monk from Bangkok, Akka Thumo the monk from Phuket, Urassaya the beautiful model from Bangkok.

Terry cheerfully said to his team. That it was time to go underground for a while leave the country go on a holiday make your-self scarce at least for the next week or so. 'I will send you a coded message when it's time to reconvene. Let' the opposition lick its wounds for a while. We will be back in plenty of time before the killings planned for the 21st of August when the Kuman Thong expect to have a bonanza day with the full moon celebration and start collecting on their initial investments.'

Akka Thumo went to his hometown in Phuket. Klahan went to his village in Samut Sakhon a small seaside province is dotted with salt and shrimp farms.

Terry Johnson went to Greece to drum up some badly needed support from the Greeks, his friend Apollo Popachki could be of great benefit for him, in procuring men arms and ammunition. He landed at Athens international airport and was met by a warm greeting by his old friend Apollo. 'How are you -you old dog, what have you gotten yourself into in Thailand eh! Come on I have a car waiting for us you can tell me about it over breakfast.' There driver took them to Syntagma square, the city's financial district with almost half of the population having to pay a visit there every day the Acropolis was also there. Apollo said Omonia square should be avoided these days because of the gangs and the pickpockets. So they went for breakfast at the safest neighborhood Plaka is known for the best area to stay the best times to go there are between March and May and from September to November. They had their breakfast in the Herodian Hotel in town the best midrange hotel in town and does a great breakfast. The two men sat at the table. They had a choice from the English breakfast to the Greek breakfast. Terry was so hungry he had a bit of both. When they had finished their breakfast and were enjoying there coffee. Apollo said 'so what do you want from me my old friend.' 'Well short of a small army I want tactical support and 100 men fully armed. To deal with a rebel group called the Kuman Thong in Thailand.' Terry then went on to explain why and what fors, he was finished with his presentation with Apollo. He said he could help him, but his men would only be able to carry handguns only NO assault riffles o.k. When do you want everything in place by? 'August the 20th and out of there in two days the 22nd at the latest. So he and his old teammate bid farewell hoping to meet in Bangkok in position on the 20th of August just one day before the Kumam Thong were believed to Strike. After a few days more days in Athens Terry Johnson also went to Paris to connect up with an old friend and colleague, from his army days, Mr. Louis Lambert. Lambert was now a top lawyer in the city of Paris. He could help bring down the perpetrators. Terry touched down in Charles de Gaulle airport, on a cold brisk Sunday morning in Paris. He was met by Louis Lambert at five-foot ten inches. He was a tall man in his late fifties with gray hair at the gills. He had nice blue eyes and a nice smile with dimples.

'Bonjour Monsieur Terry Johnson.' 'Good morning your-self Louis, how the devil are you doing yourself?' They gave each other a big bear hug and decided to go foe breakfast at the Rue Vernet brasserie and café. Not far from the Arc de Triomphe. Ater explaining the current situation to the lawyer Terry wanted to know how he could arrest the men responsible for these Human rights atrocities and bring them to justice. There was a silence between them, Louis broke the silence. 'Well Monsieur Terry the best way is to issue an international arrest warrant in the names of the perpetrators and apply for an extradition request from

Thailand to the Hague. Thailand may refuse to Extradite the Perpetrators to Europe, in which case you will have lost them. However, if they were suddenly found to be in France or another part a Europe they could be arrested and be placed in a European jail to await their Trials on Human rights issues in the Hague. But if the fugitives decide to fight off the extradition request it could take years to go through the law courts in Thailand, and the international criminal courts of the Hague.

Terry Johson then spoke. 'What if the fugitives decided to voluntarily surrender themselves to European arrest warrants would that work?' 'Louis replied and how do you expect them to volunteer to surrender. These are hardened criminals with track records as long as your arms.

There may be a way to get them to volunteer to surrender themselves to The European Arrest warrant.' 'Let me think about that one, 'said Terry.

They bid there farewells and promised to keep in touch should anything develop further down the line. A word of warning Terry said Louis. 'The fugitives are supposed to come by there own volition you are not allowed to force them in any way. Terry just nodded without saying anything. The trip to Europe was very fruitful. The next day he flew back to Thailand where he would be reunited with his friends and fight his enemies.

He had a coffee morning with what was left of his his associates in the early hours near the floating market at Damnoen Saduak. How are we doing today? said Terry. Each person in the group reported about their own lock down experience. And they gave a unanimous vote that they were ready for action and anything that the Kuman Thong were about to throw at them.

Chapter-Sixteen

Terry's Gang of four were all back together again. Planning the next stage of their attack on the Kuman Thong. They also heard through the vine that their leader Channarong was released from the Hospital. Their secretary Sakda was alive and well and so was Anurak their hit man. The 21st of August was fast approaching so they needed a good plan to put into action.

We will be having 100 armed militias from Greece to join us in the fight against the Kuman Thong. 'How many men have the Kuman Thong got?' asked Klahan. 'About 1000 plus I should think, 'Replied Terry, adding, 'But they are not trained like our 100 men from Greece are.'

It was Channarong who made the first move by sending about two hundred armed men against Terrys gang inside the Wat Pho Temple. But they were quickly stopped when the 500 or so monks closed the heavy foot thick doors and locked them out. It was now practically a siege.

Then suddenly there was the unmistakable sound of gunfire outside the temple. It was Apollo the (Greek) and his merry men attacking the Kuman Thong from the rear, and it was working. The crowds of men who sieged the gates of the Wat Pho Temple dispersed. Terry ordered the gates to be opened as it was now safe from the Kuman Thong. Then the 100 men strong flowed through the gates smiling and unharmed. Several bodies of the Kuma Thong lay outside the gates. Terry ordered that they leave them alone as a warning to other Kuman Thong not to try that maneuver again.

Terry said, 'Since the Kuman Thong's H.Q. Wat Na Thong Nok Temple was destroyed in the Blast of the bombing. Notwithstanding the bombing of the Golf Club. The Kuman Thong had to find a new H.Q. 'This was quickly found out by his gang to be the Massive new warehouse blocks at 'Sermsuk warehouses 721 Charoen Nakhon road. The warehouses on that road were all being turned into hospital beds about 3000 plus of them maybe more. At $10.000 a pop that's 30 million dollars return on their investment. It was fast approaching the 21st of August, so we've got to be ready,' finished Terry.

Terry Johnson met up with Apollo Papachi in a coffee shop called the factory coffee in 49 Phaya Thai road. In the center of town it was very crowded so it would be difficult to spot them. Terry said, 'Thanks for arriving early in Bangkok, we might have been toast if you hadn't got there in time to stop them entering the Temple.'

'Not at all, not at all, my friend we heard rumors that after what you'd done to them in the bombing of their H.Q. a counter attack was imminent. Because of the constant bodyguards It was going to be hard to get at their leader Channarong. I want him to be extradited to the Hague for his crimes against humanity,' said Terry. 'Good luck with that,' said Apollo, adding, 'he will have the Judges on his side so they will refuse the extradition request made from the Hague. What if he Volunteered to go willingly to the Hague, 'said Terry. To go willingly as in volunteer to go with you to the Hague, to face what might be a life sentence. You've got to be joking man. No way that would happen, no way.'

'I have to find a way to get him into a proper court of law to face judgement,' said Terry. Suddenly, Terry spotted a red dot of blood on Apollos forehead. Hed been shot by a sniper bang in the middle of his forehead. Apollo slumped forwards his head banged on the table. He was dead. Terry quickly left the scene before any police arrived. He ran a couple of blocks down Khaosan Road and across to the fish market, where there were plenty of people for cover.

He met his people back at Wat Pho Temple. Klahan, Akka Thumo, and

Urassaya. All waiting for new orders to do. With what was left of the crew and Apollos men although Apollo left plans behind him incase of his early demise. He put a man called Dimitri's in charge he was a big man with a thick mustache wiry hair, a big bulbous nose, thick lips, and dark green eyes.

Dimitris met up with Terry at the Wat Pho Temple where it was safe. They went to the small prayer room where they always met. Terry introduced his Greek friend to the rest of the team. They were all happy to meet Dimitris knowing he had control over 100 Greek armed men made them feel a little more secure.

Sakda the Kuman Thong's secretary suddenly turned up at the Wat Pho Temple asking for Terry Johnson. He was waving a small white flag in front of him. Terry was weary of meeting him but decided that because he had a white flag of truce in front of him, he decided to meet him.

Sakda was a huge fat man of about 150 kilos with a bald head of a monk and the duty orange robes. 'What is the meaning of this truce,' said Terry to the fat man.

Sakda spoke loudly, 'Since our leader Channarong is still a little unwell. I have been temporarily put in charge of the whole of the Kuman Thong. I have been given the authority to deal with the day-to-day running's of our organization as well as making the major decisions on what to do next. It seems we are at an impasse, where neither side can move ahead with their plans.'

'We know that you have plans for the 21st of August. But for what exactly, for we don't know.' 'Would you like to enlighten me?' said Terry.

'I am not at liberty to tell you what we are going to do on 21st of August.'

'Isn't that the day that you hope to relieve up to 3000 women who are in their seventh- or eighth-month pregnancy with their babies?' said Terry.

'You can't stop it! It is written down by our forefathers. We have been practicing this ritual for hundreds of years. It is a part of our culture,' said Sakda the fat monk.

Terry replied, 'This so-called ritual that you do, is nothing more than organized murder. The women are seven or eight months pregnant, and we've found out that form of caesarean section often kills the woman which makes it a double murder. On top of that you sell the woman's baby fetus for $10.000.'

'Well if you try and stop it, strange things will start to happen to you and harm you. It's called bad Karma. Accidents will be regular and more obvious. Illness may overcome you, strangers will come up to you and attack you for no reason. You will be prone to crash your car into a head on collisions. Things may fall on top of your head as you walk down the street. Buses cars or trains may run over you for no reason. Your friends will suddenly turn on you and become your enemies. Bad luck will be your middle name.'

'We don't believe in any of that Karma stuff or spirits of any kind. O.K. fat man,' said Terry.

Sakda bellowed, 'As we speak the witch doctors that survived the bombings are making spells of bad karma with their existing Baby spirits of the Kuman Thong. They are going to attack you in many ways. I have been sent to warn you not to interfere with our abortion plans and ask you to stay away from it. Or it will only bring serious harm to you and your family members.'

Terry said, 'Well, I am going to do my best to see that you put a stop to this abominable practice of yours and put the likes of you out of business. You and your friends will face justice and go to jail for the rest of your life. Get out of my Temple fat man before I have you thrown out.'

The fat man's face went red with frustration. He quickly turned around and walked out briskly the way he came in shaking his head in anger and despair. As he returned to the warehouses at 721 Charoen Nakhon road. He knew that his boss Channarong would not be a happy man at all.

Chapter-Seventeen

Bad things have already started to happen, Terry thought, but we won't let anybody know what has happened.

A big piece of scaffolding fell from a skyscraper and hit the ground just missing Urassaya by inches.

A car came around the corner and braked hard then skidded before it hit Akka Thumo in the shin's but no broken bones only bruises.

A total stranger came up to Klahan and spat at him in the face, for no reason at all.

Terry was crossing the road at a Zebra crossing when a motor biker ran the red light and clipped Terry's arm spinning him round to the ground.

Was this the Kuman Thong in action, who knows? Terry told everyone to be on their guard, just in case.

Back at H.Q things happened there too but it won't be told for fear of it sounding ridiculous. What can be said is that windows were braking, doors slamming, locking themselves, candles blowing themselves out. From nowhere a gale force wind was running through the complex. Then all of a sudden there was silence.

Terry gathered everyone in the small prayer room to give each person their instructions for tomorrow as it was the 21st of August the big day for the Kuman Thongs Abortion day.

We must do some planning for tomorrow, the 21ST of August.

Firstly, Akka Thumo you must go to Pramuan road to pick up the Prostitute, Sherine. You will have the protection of at least 10 of Dimitris men with Glock handguns to watch your back.

Secondly, Klahan you will go with Urassaya who will look eight months pregnant. You will play her pimp. After being picked up, she will be our girl on the inside. She will open the doors of the warehouses so we may gain access to the main warehouse and attack the guards at warehouse one. You will also have 10 men from Dimitris bearing Glock pistols, for your protection. We also have six buses and 50 tuk tuks at our disposal.

Terry and Dimitris said they would pick up the dozen or so women from the up-market Kaze coffee shop on Prauan road. Bring them all here to the Wat

Pho Temple for protection. Then join up with the rest of Dimitris men and attack the guards at the warehouses at 721 Charoen Nakhan road.

All of the other women who want protection from the Kuman Thong should join the other ladies transport to the Wat Pho Temple.

The remaining armed men of Dimitris gang will surround the warehouses to prevent anyone escaping. Operation abortion was now in action.

0.60am on the 21st of August. Channarong the Kuman Thong leader was sipping coffee with his favorite men around him. They were Sakda his personal secretary and Anurak, his hit man. 'Are we all set to have a most profitable day today gentlemen?' 'Yes we are sir,' said Sakda, 'we have over

1000 men all in position guarding the warehouse's and 500 men to collect the whores. 100 abortion doctors all ready for action. 3000 beds for the whores to be tied to if necessary. Yes boss all is now ready.'

'Good Sakda, 'very good. And what will you be doing hit man?'

Anurak said that he would be on the roof tops of the warehouses, taking pot shots at the enemy. 'No problem I expect to kill at least a 100 today if not more, ha.' He had a little chuckle to himself.

At seven am Akka Thuma made his way in a tuk, tuk, over to Silmon 15 Alley where he saw a woman waiting for him by the road side. He told the tuk tuk driver to turn around and wait. 'Are you ready Sherine?' asked Akka

Thumo. 'Morning sir. I'm so glad to see you!' 'Climb on board, 'said Akka Thumo. As she was about to board the tuk tuk, a man came out of nowhere with a big knife in his hand and said, 'Hoy you, whore, where do you think you're going?' And made steps toward the girl as she was trying to climb on board the tuk tuk, When all of a sudden there was a loud bang! Akka Thumo wasn't taking any chances he took out his Glock and shot the intruder right between his eyes. Dead.

Then they set off for the Wat Phu Temple. The first woman of operation abortion had been saved.

Next up was the beautiful but pregnant Urassaya partnered up with the stocky looking Klahan from Phuket. They both made tracks to the fish market, and immediately met up with the rich looking businessman, saying 'Arh you've arrived at last. I've been waiting for you since six am.' 'Well we are here now so shouldn't we get on with it?' said Klahan. As soon as she got into the back of a black Mercedes, a shot rang out and the fat rich looking business man fell to the ground. He was shot by one of Demetris's men. They were under strict instructions not to take any prisoners. And they took their jobs very seriously indeed. The driver took off before Urassaya got in the car leaving her stranded on the pavement. She screamed, 'You fucking idiots. You were supposed to let me go, so that I could unlock the warehouse doors from the inside!' She ripped off her pregnancy gear she was wearing and stormed off to the Wat Pho Temple to see if she could do any better over there.

Terry and Dimitris went straight to the up-market Kaze coffee shop to collect as many women as possible that wanted to go free of charge. When they arrived on pramuan road, he could see a crowd of women all waiting outside the up-market Kaze coffee shop for a lift out of here to the safety of the Wat Pho Temple. They did meet some opposition to their cause, but these problems were quickly snuffed out by Demetrius's men and their Glocks.

They did several trips to the red-light districts to collect hundreds of pregnant girls of all ages and sizes. With only a few skirmishes with the untrained opposition. It was getting late in the day when the final tally of pregnant women were counted up, but they had gone well over two thousand by six p.m.

By contrast the warehouses at the 721 Chaaroen Nakhan road were relatively empty. With Idle doctors standing by but no patients to perform their crude methods of cesarean section operations at all. The guards outside the warehouses had nothing to do but sit around and twiddle their thumbs.

Operation abortion had been successful there were very few casualties. Only those women who were most determined to end their pregnancies.

In a secret location somewhere in the city was the boss of the Kuman Thong. Together with his minions. He was livid, fuming, hopping, mad about the results he was out of pocket by millions. After paying the doctors and the guards the empty beds, The empty warehouses. Especially all the $1000 dollars he paid for each girl for an abortion so he could get his $10,000 baby spirit's reward.

The end for now!

Authors notation

Yes this is a fictional story that tells you that the operation abortion was a success. But the baddies are always out there lurking in the shadows all over the land where the Kuman Thong exists. And that was on the admission of a high-ranking monk who I personally interviewed in Thailand recently and, like me, would like to see an end to this practice of late abortions for baby spirits, abolished in Buddhism forever.

Harry J Blackwood.

With Apollo Papadaki dead and Dimitri taken over will the French Lawyer Louis Lambert with the help of Terry

Johnson bring the perpetrators by way of extradition to the criminal court of justice in the Hague for crimes against humanity. Extradition was one subject Terry Johnson knew all about. See in Harry J. Blackwood's next book.

Printed in the United States
by Baker & Taylor Publisher Services